TreeHouse

1430 W. Susquehanna Ave
Philadelphia, PA 19121
215-236-1760 | treehousebooks.org

SUMMER TUNES

A Martha's Vineyard Vacation

by Patricia McMahon
Photographs by Peter Simon

BOYDS MILLS PRESS

ACKNOWLEDGMENTS

I want to say a most sincere and heartfelt (honest!) thank you to the Healys, for saying yes, for sharing their vacation, for putting up with the aggro, and for being swell guys, one and all.

Particular thanks to Mr. Conor Healy, Esquire, for all his assistance, for sharing his thoughts, for his willingness to attend business meetings, for one of the nicest waterside lunches I have ever had.

I send my thanks to Barbara Dacey, and all the staff at WMVY.

I have to express my gratitude to the women of the Friday Club, stalwart friends all, who aided and abetted me in the complicated arrangements necessary for the Vineyard excursion. Special honors and awards go to Martha Davis, who rises above and beyond, and who brought what I needed to the ferry.

I would like to thank Jean Lamere for understanding the concept of a friend in need (okay—Kent, too) and providing extraordinary assistance.

I would like to mention Fred Hurley and the staff of the Laurel Inn, Edgartown, who kept the calls and the kindness coming.

I would like to thank the faculty, staff, administration, parents, and students of the Wolfe Elementary School, Katy Independent School District, who made us feel so welcome in Houston while I wrote this book.

Kind assistance was provided, as always, by Joseph McCarthy, my twenty-year man, and by Conor Clarke McCarthy, the intrepid traveler who now knows too much about being ill in an inn. I do now, and always, appreciate their support—and that of Nellie, who waits while I write.

Published by Caroline House
Boyds Mills Press, Inc.
A Highlights Company
815 Church Street
Honesdale, Pennsylvania 18431
Printed in Mexico

Publisher Cataloging-in-Publication Data
McMahon, Patricia.
Summer Tunes: A Martha's Vineyard Vacation / by Patricia McMahon;
full-color photography by Peter Simon.—1st ed. [48]p. : col. ill. ; cm.
Summary : Ten-year-old Conor, who has cerebral palsy, spends a summer
vacation with his family on Martha's Vineyard in this photographic essay.
ISBN 1-56397-572-6
1. Martha's Vineyard (Mass)—Biography—Juvenile literature.
2. Cerebral palsied children—Biography—Juvenile literature.
[1. Martha's Vineyard (Mass). —Biography.
2. Cerebral palsied children—Biography.] I. Simon, Peter, ill. II. Title.
917.44   [B]—dc20   1996   AC   CIP
Library of Congress Catalog Card Number 95-83980

First edition, 1996
Book designed by Amy Drinker, Aster Designs
The text of this book is set in 13.5 point Janson.
10   9   8   7   6   5   4   3   2   1

For a sister and two brothers—
Marissa, Brendan and Joshua Spears—
and
for a brother and two sisters—
Conor, Carrie and Brenna Healy
(lucky me, they're all my friends).
— *P.M.*

To Conor Healy—
for all the joy and good feelings he shares.
— *P.S.*

Thanks to my loving family for helping me through hard times;
to Nana, my friend and supporter;
to Joe Frese, S.J. (my namesake),
and Jamie Capetta, my Catholic brothers;
and to Jo Bisson, my bus driver and dear, daily friend.
— *Conor Healy*

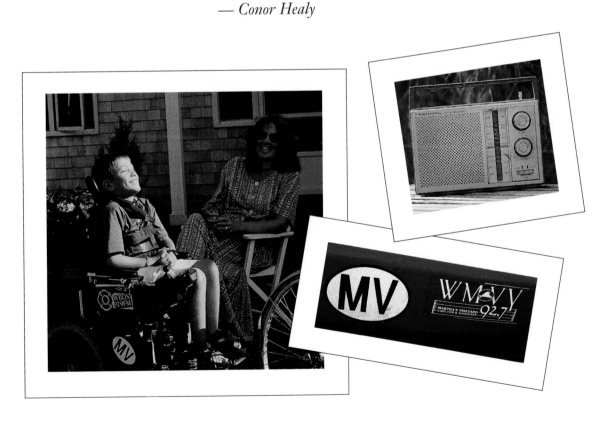

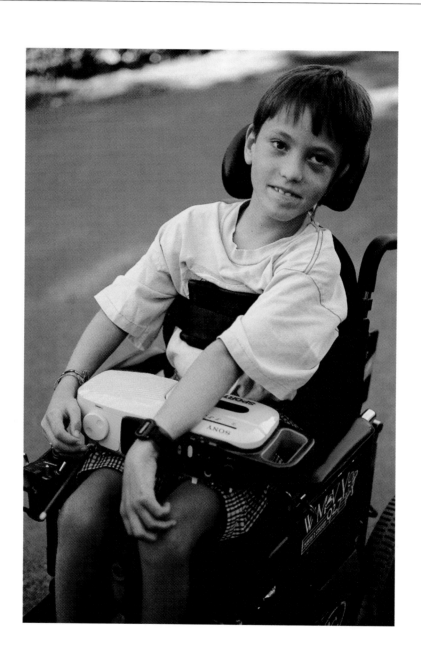

On this hot August morning, the music from the radio matches the feeling of the day. Conor Healy smiles, enjoying the *shu-bop, shu-bop* of the backbeat as the words "in the summertime" fill the van. Music, music, and the right words, for the right time, in perfect sync with the day—there's nothing ten-year-old Conor likes better.

The highway flashing by the window leads away from home in Concord, Massachusetts, to Cape Cod—where there is a ferry going to the island of Martha's Vineyard, the Healy family destination.

Conor's mother, Joan, drums her fingers on the steering wheel as she drives, picking up the beat as well. Brenna, Conor's four-year-old sister, fills the whole back seat with crayons, papers, books, and her necessary Baba, which was once a sheep but now resembles a woolly pile with legs.

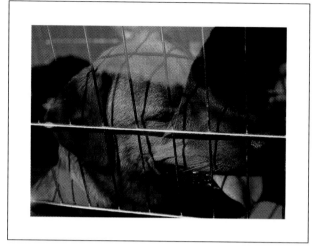

"I'm waving to Hershey," Brenna tells Conor, "and he's waving back. Do you see, do you see?" Brenna points to the Jeep ahead, the lead vehicle in the Healy family vacation caravan. Conor's father, Tom, drives his two passengers—Conor's eleven-year-old sister, Carrie, and Hershey, the dog.

As the song ends, Conor tells his mother which song the DJ will play next. Joan is sure he'll be right. And he is. When it comes to music, Conor's family is surprised only if he is wrong. But the next song is barely heard as Joan turns down a small hill and Conor yells, "Ferry!" with all his might.

A long line of cars, trucks, jeeps, vans, bicycles, and people slowly move in turn into the giant hole in the ferry's middle. Brenna loudly counts blue cars. Carrie waves back from the Jeep, while Hershey looks

like he would rather be running than riding. On the radio, a Cape Cod DJ announces Conor's favorite new song, sung by a band named for a fish. *A beach song*, Conor thinks, *that's what I would play next.*

Holding down the button on the outside of the van, Joan lowers the van's ramp into the only spot on the ferry where there's room for it, and Conor drives his chair onto the elevator.

With a mournful Hershey left behind, the Healy family makes its way to a table out in the summer-bright sun. Brenna covers her ears as the ferry sounds a horribly loud "We're-going-now" noise. Seagulls sing a hungry song, floating low, waiting to catch the bread and cookies they know people will throw. A portable radio serves up a Jimmy Buffett song. *Yes!* thinks Conor. *Beach music!* It's so satisfying when he and a DJ agree. The sky is blue, blue. The water is sprinkled with sailboats. And Martha's Vineyard lies out there, waiting.

Time on the ferry, like vacation time, seems to float by so slowly, yet be over so quickly. The boat moves steadily out to sea as the Healys' conversation turns toward Vineyard plans. Excited to be nearing their island home, the family talks about boats, beaches, bicycles, family visits, and piles of books to be read.

Carrie thinks of the writing she wants to do, Brenna plans to find a million shells, and Conor talks of the radio station he can't wait to visit. Brenna dances just out of reach, but close enough to catch. Carrie decides to join the long cold-drinks line. Conor

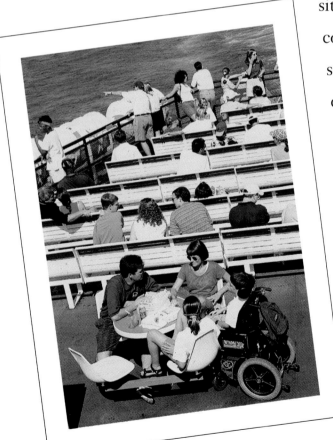

sits, listening to the sounds of radios competing with the hum of conversation, the laughter of students crowded around a small table, the steady whirr of the engines, and the shouts of a small boy who yells, "Boat!" every time he sees one of the oh-so-many boats on Vineyard Sound.

It's a vacation song that carries on as Tom and Conor decide to take a walk together around the boat.

Most, but not all, people use their legs to get around. Conor Healy uses a wheelchair. He has one that his family and friends can push, but he prefers to drive himself in his electric one. He pushes a round knob to control the chair's movements, forward or backward, slowly or not.

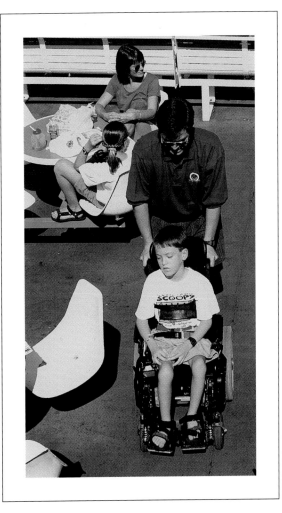

The wheelchair helps Conor move because his muscles do not. Conor has something called cerebral palsy. When Conor was born, he was born too early. Because he was too early and too small, he had some problems. One problem bothered part of his brain—the part that tells his muscles what to do.

Although Conor is healthy now, the connection between one part of his brain and his muscles doesn't work. But that's the only part of Conor's brain with a problem. The rest works very well, indeed. Anyone who wants to test the memory part of his or her brain against Conor Healy's had better be prepared to lose. And the song-knowing and song-loving parts of Conor's brain are in first-class working order.

The ferry whistle announces loudly, "We're here!" Everyone clamors into cars—ready to go. The Healys add their small caravan to the long line winding its way into the Vineyard's narrow streets. The Jeep and the van turn left at the sign for Edgartown. Everyone is glad to be back.

"Martha's Vineyard" may seem a strange name for an island. Last year Carrie, being curious, found out that although there is more than one theory of how the Vineyard was named, most historians believe that the English explorer Bartholomew Gosnold named the island for his baby daughter, Martha—growing bigger every day, far away in England. He added the "Vineyard" part because of the profusion of wild grapes he found there. He did not name the Vineyard for the people of the Wampanoag Nation, who were already living there and probably keeping a close eye, indeed, on Mr. Gosnold.

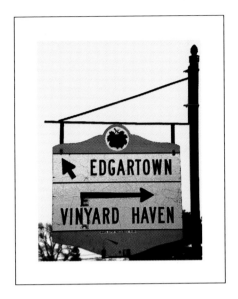

Martha's Vineyard used to be famous for whaling until the whaling business came to an end. This was good news for the whales, but not for the people of the island who had lost their way of making a living.

Because the island is so lovely, visitors began to come to the Vineyard for summer vacations. Presidents like Ulysses S. Grant and Bill Clinton have come to relax from the big job of being president. Writers have come to write their books, musicians to write their songs. Families of all sizes, shapes, and colors come to stay in houses grand or cottages simple and small.

As the Healys drive into Edgartown, they pass a sign saying WMVY. "All right!" calls Conor. "Turn up the radio."

Then comes the left turn, and a right, and they're at their island home. The Healys own a small house, with all the rooms on one floor. There's a ramp at the side door for Conor's wheel-chair, and another ramp at the back. The house is close enough to Edgartown center so Carrie and Conor can head there them-selves—big kids on their own.

First things first, however. Everything that was loaded into the cars in Concord must now be unloaded. Tom and Joan set to work. Conor steers out of the way, heading inside to turn the radio dial to exactly the right spot. Brenna dashes about. Carrie, glad to be here, pitches in. Hershey, finding a small spot of shade, settles in the grass to recover from the journey.

To cheer everyone on in their work, Conor cranks up the volume. The radio is tuned to WMVY, the island radio station and Conor's favorite place on the Vineyard. Stickers from WMVY, as well as from Boston and Concord radio stations, adorn his wheelchair. At home, Conor has his CD player, and he loves to pretend to be a DJ— programming songs, interrupting for commercials and announcements.

On the Vineyard, Conor has his bright yellow boom-box. He also has his favorite DJ—Barbara Dacey. He and Barbara met by phone when Conor called to say how much he liked the way she mixed and matched songs. The two became friends. Friends visit one another, so Conor went to the station last summer. He loved it. And he wants to go again.

There are, however, oh-so-many places to go and other sounds the Healys want to hear— such as the sound of waves slapping against a boat as it moves through the water.

So before any trip to the station, there will be an adventure tomorrow morning on *Canora*, the Healys' boat. *Canora* sits moored in the harbor, surrounded by boats that look big enough to have sailed Mr. Gosnold and all his family from England. Carrie, Conor, and Brenna named *Canora* for themselves: *CA* for Carrie, *NOR* for Conor, and the final *A* for Brenna.

The very first thing next morning, Captain Tom brings *Canora* to the town dock for his family. Wheelchairs aren't the best in boats, but Joan has a blue chair which holds Conor comfortably. Carrie likes taking charge of tying up the boat. With a little of this and some of that, the family and their gear are soon aboard. Tom, who is new to the skills of boating, steers carefully as Carrie warns him of anything and everything he is going to hit.

Missing all boats, beacons, and buoys, Tom heads out of Edgartown Harbor toward Vineyard Sound. Carrie rides on the bow, happily bouncing on the waves, forgetting to remind her father that he cannot steer. The sunlight makes diamond patterns on the water. Carrie imagines a story that

14

begins with a girl setting foot on one of those watery paths.
Brenna sets up house in the small cabin, which she says is hers.
No one can come in—unless the person says "Please."

Conor laughs as they hit the wake from other boats, sure that Carrie will fly off the boat or that his chair will fly off the seat. Joan sits in the back doing the important job of relaxing while constantly counting to make sure everyone is still aboard.

The Vineyard lies lovely in the sun, looking as it must have long ago to Bartholomew Gosnold. Except that back then there were no shingled houses, no docks, no lighthouses, no power boats or sailboats. No ferry, either. If all of that had been there, it would have surprised Mr. Gosnold so much that the Healys might now be sailing around "Surprise Island."

Conor takes his turn at the wheel.

"All right, Buddy, you can do it," Tom assures him.

All hands prepare for disaster, Carrie thinks. As he steers, Conor carefully monitors the ship-to-shore radio, which plays no Rolling Stones and today has no shipwrecks to announce. As time passes, Tom reclaims the helm while Conor and Carrie begin to argue about which song is better—the one Conor likes, sung by the fish band, or the one Carrie likes, sung by the woman who always sounds as if she's in a bad mood. Brenna decides she wants to get off the boat *now* and is not deterred by any explanation of the distance from ship to shore.

Captain Tom Healy decides to head
back to shore before the crew mutinies.
Joan leads a discussion of how big a dent
Tom will make in the town dock.

The captain feels his seaworthy
skills are greatly underestimated.
All the gulls in town seem to line
up on the dock to see how he
does—which turns out to be better
than all right. A friendly lady in a
straw hat helps Carrie tie up.
Carrie didn't need or want help,
but what can you do about friendly
ladies in straw hats?

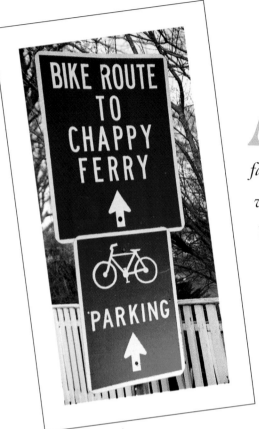

And what can you do, Conor Healy wonders the next day, *about a family who wants to go to the beach instead of wait while I visit a radio station?* Nothing, but go along and have some fun.

"We have to have an official day at the beach. We're on vacation," Tom reminds everyone. Conor and Carrie do not find this an earthshaking news bulletin.

After a fast loading-up of the Jeep, they head down through Edgartown. "Edgar" was not another child of Bartholomew Gosnold, but in fact the nephew of the king of England. In 1671, early colonists thought that if they named the town for the king's favorite nephew, the king would think they were a swell bunch and help them if they needed it. Unfortunately, Edgar died about the time they named the town—but the name remains.

On the waterfront in Edgartown is the dock for the Chappaquiddick ferry. The *On Time* is a small ferry that runs back and forth across the harbor from early morning until late at night. She carries passengers and cars to Chappaquiddick, which is clearly not named for royal children.

Tom stops to let air out of the tires so the Jeep can drive on sand. He heads off the paved roads and right onto the beach. Here, there is peace and quiet. Here, they can have their own Healy family party. Here, Conor can go straight from the car into the blue chair, which fits in a beach chair. This is so much easier than struggling to do the impossible: push a wheelchair through sand.

Joan covers everyone in suntan lotion. Mothers do that. Conor grimaces as she does. Kids do that.

Carrie runs as fast as she can into the surf, then back out again. "It's cold!" she says. But not too cold—because she dives right back in again, followed by Tom.

Brenna begins collecting shells, aided by Joan in this important job. Conor turns up the music, beach-loud. He calls to tell Carrie that the depressed singer is about to complain again. But still Conor sings along happily in his slow Conor way.

Muscles are not only needed for arms and legs—they are in faces as well. Conor's speech is slow as he struggles to make his mouth say the

many important and interesting thoughts in his brain. He always wins the struggle, as long as the listener is patient.

Once someone is used to Conor's way of talking, it's easy to understand him. And there is never any problem understanding his laugh, which is strong and loud now as he watches Carrie tumble over, knocked down by a wave.

A beach day passes for Conor and for all the Healys. They move slowly from beach work to beach work: playing toss, lying in the sun, listening to the ocean as it tells its story, leaning against Dad as the surf washes over, laughing as the sand sucks away underfoot, lying in the sun again, listening to beach music, singing along, enjoying the day. Finally they head home, feeling gritty, tired, and extra hungry, with the windows open and everyone happy that the music is loud.

While waiting for the

On Time, Carrie says to everyone, "Look who's over there."

"It's Mrs. Nasty Despicable!" Conor cries.

"Despicable, despicable," Brenna chants.

They met her last year in Edgartown, when she was carefully parking her car in a spot marked for cars with special needs—like the need to have enough space to let a ramp down. Because Mrs. Nasty had no special plate, Joan asked her nicely to park in some other place.

Mrs. Nasty started to yell at Joan: *Why* did Joan have that plate on her car? *Why* did she need that spot? *Where* was Joan going, and *who* did she think she was?

22

"That woman...she was despicable," Joan said after the lady left.

"Nasty despicable," Carrie added.

"Mrs. Nasty Despicable," Conor said.

"Despicable, despicable," Brenna shouted, until they all laughed and weren't mad anymore. Now, whenever someone parks in a special spot for no reason, the Healys know who it is: Mrs. Nasty Despicable. Or Mister.

Watching her go, Conor tries to decide what song he would play if he were a DJ and someone called to dedicate a song to Mrs. Nasty Despicable.

The next day, Conor decides to dedicate a song to himself—a song for a kid who wants to go to a radio station and never gets there. Some other vacation plans always seem to come first. Conor can't go today because company's coming in the afternoon. Conor listens to Barbara Dacey, wishing she would play Van Morrison's "Brown-eyed Girl." Then he could start the day with his favorite singer *and* his favorite song. But Sting comes up, with a promise of U2. *Well, all right*, Conor concedes as he leaves the music behind.

A Vineyard vacation isn't officially underway until the Healys have breakfast at the Dock Street Coffee Shop. On their way, Carrie talks about her story; it will have a heroine named Caroline, who walks across a path of sunlight on the water, which leads back in time on Martha's Vineyard. Conor sometimes

wishes he could sit up high, joining his
family for breakfast at the counter. But
there's no way to reach it except by sitting
on a stool, which he can't do. Still, the eggs
are great, the owners are swell, and the radio
plays loud enough for everyone to hear. At
least it's Van Morrison—even if it's not
"Brown-eyed Girl."

After breakfast, they wander through the streets of Edgartown. Brenna takes rides when she can; the streets are long and lead uphill. The family stops in front of the church where Joan and Tom were married. Since they came from different parts of the United States, Joan and Tom decided to be married in the most beautiful place they knew—right here in Edgartown. They've been coming back ever since.

The family finds a bench for leg-resting and people-watching. Window-shopping has to do for the Healys most of the time.

Few shops have ramps, so there aren't many Conor can enter on his own. He knows that the narrow sidewalks and steep old steps of the Vineyard stores would make it hard to add ramps—but having some would be nice.

Then it's home again, home again, for there's work to be done: sweeping away the constant sand, making salads, and changing dirty T-shirts.

Conor, steering clear of the hubbub, drives his chair up and down the street, enjoying his own company, listening to the police band radio strapped to his chair. A policeman in Concord gave Conor his first police radio. When the winters are cold and the snows are high, Conor still knows a great deal about what is going on in town. Actually, as Joan points out, he usually knows what's going *wrong* in town.

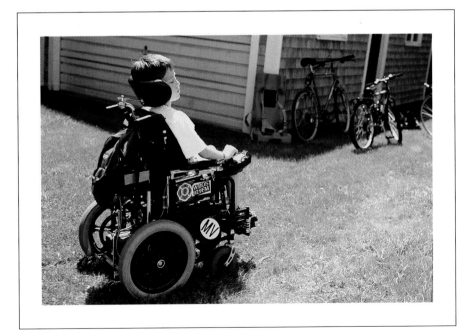

Finally the
guests arrive, and
it's high-fives from
a distant cousin and
a few kisses as well.
The grown-ups begin
to talk about everyone
and everything. Conor,
Carrie, and Brenna get
to know cousin Beth's
boys. Soon everyone is
trading stories and
favorite family facts. The
grown-ups sit around chat-
ting, which never seems as
much fun to Conor and
Carrie as it does to the
grown-ups.

Tom lights the grill and
takes orders. Hershey would
like a burger but will settle
for a hot dog. Brenna

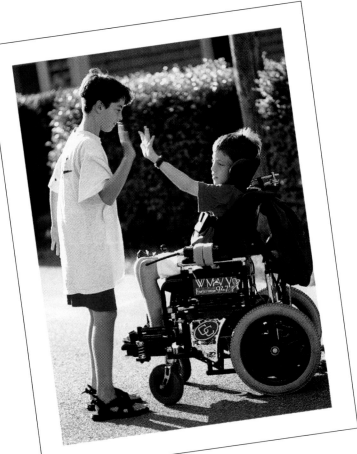

splashes in the pool and gets a
new friend to join her. Everyone
crowds around the table, finding
space to eat, keeping the story
hum going. Conor trades
laughs out front with a friend
who's stopped by to visit. The
afternoon slips into evening.
Hershey sings a sad dog
song about hamburgers
he's never had. The visi-
tors head toward home.
One day slides into
another.

And another....On one of those days the whole family goes to Oak Bluffs for a ride on the Flying Horses, the oldest working carousel in America. Tom and Conor race happily around together trying to catch the brass ring.

And on another day Tom and Conor go to the Gay Head cliffs, on the island's western edge. The Wampanoags called the area Aquinnah. Mr. Gosnold called it Land Under the Hills, which was descriptive, but not as interesting as some of the other names he chose. Tom and Conor find a sitting place. Conor listens to the sound of the waves hitting the cliffs, and enjoys a quiet moment of not trying to get anywhere in particular.

Finally, one morning, Tom tells Conor to give the radio station a call, and they'll ride over. The call goes through, and Barbara Dacey tells Conor she'd love to see him, but it will have to be any day other than today—how about tomorrow?

Conor really wanted to go *today*. He bangs his hand on the table in frustration, which is not the softest or the loveliest of vacation sounds. Carrie doesn't see what the big deal is and says so, which is not the friend-liest of vacation sounds.

Conor gets mad at Carrie, which convinces Joan that the family needs to get out of the house and onto their bicycles. So—no arguing—they load up.

Carrie rides her own bicycle while Brenna happily rides in a seat behind Joan. Conor looks flash in his bright

yellow Conor-mobile, a trailer pulled
behind Tom, with the yellow radio
strapped in beside him. They ride
through the town, down to the harbor, heading toward the lighthouse.
Carrie and Conor's frustration
fades as the pleasure of the ride
takes over. A few heads turn as
Conor goes by with his music
blaring, taking in the summer
scene, listening to summer tunes.

The ride almost works the magic of changing moods—until they stop for a moment in town. And then it happens to Conor, again. While they're discussing which way to go, Conor notices a lady staring. She crosses over to him, smiling kindly, her hand in her pocketbook. *Oh no*, Conor thinks, *here we go again.*

"Oh no," Joan says quietly. "Here we go again."

Carrie sees the woman, and decides to ride ahead as if she is on her own.

The lady, who is surely a nice lady, gives Conor some money. "For buying some ice cream," she says.

Tom leans back, telling Conor, "Don't worry about it, Buddy," as they continue on their ride.

But Conor does worry about it. *I'm mad*, he thinks. *She just feels sorry for me*, he knows. He thinks of all the things he would like to say to the lady who gave him money.

He knows it wouldn't be nice, but he'd like to say, "Why don't you give it to someone who needs it?" He wonders if he should just ask, "Hey, do you feel sorry for me?" and then say, "Well don't, okay?" He wants to say, "Hey, I get around the way I get around," and to ask, "How would you like it if I felt sorry for you because of the way you looked?" But Conor doesn't say those things. He never has. Riding around, angry, he thinks, *I'm getting ready to, though. One more dollar, one more dollar, and—BOOM—I'll explode.*

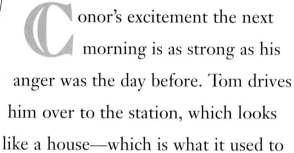

Conor's excitement the next morning is as strong as his anger was the day before. Tom drives him over to the station, which looks like a house—which is what it used to be—except this house has an odd-looking antenna and a large parking lot. The front door has those wheelchair-stopping steps, but Tom pulls Conor in. Everyone at the station remembers Conor. They call out greetings and slap high-fives.

The walls are covered with posters of people who make music, singers whose faces everyone knows, bands whose songs Conor knows by heart. Tom pushes Conor through a narrow hall filled with more pictures of singers, singers everywhere.

They go through a heavy door, and then he's right in the broadcasting booth with Barbara Dacey—live, on the air. Conor reminds Tom for the tenth time that he'll have to be quiet while Barbara's talking. Otherwise the island listeners will hear them.

Barbara sits surrounded by tapes, CDs, music machines, a phone for listeners like Conor to reach her, copy to be read, announcements to be made, and a microphone to carry her voice to listeners. While a song plays, Conor and Barbara catch up on news. Conor lets her know he's excited to hear she has been nominated for a "DJ of the Year" award. She's pretty excited, too. There's a CD Barbara thinks Conor would like, so he'll be going home with some new music.

When it's time for Barbara to talk, it's time for quiet in the booth. Utterly happy, Conor knows this is what he wants to do someday. He watches Barbara as she works from her chair. Not walking at all, not using many muscles, she is able to go out to homes, to breakfast restaurants, to beaches, and even to a bicycle trailer being pulled around town. She chooses the songs to play, and those songs can help a listener loosen his or her

anger, laugh with a sister,
remember a third-grade
teacher, or travel with a song
to a place he or she might
rather be. Conor cannot
think of any work he
would rather do.

Conor would love to
stay all day, but that's
not possible. As he and
Tom are leaving, someone stops them to say
he's called a musician friend of his, telling her about Conor and
how much he loves music. Would Conor like to meet her?

"Great!" Conor says.

"Why not?" says Tom.

The directions lead them this way and that to Carly Simon's
door—where Conor tells her he likes her music and that he once
had to call a Boston DJ who had announced the wrong title for
one of her songs and how he hoped he might be able to get a
ticket to see her in concert this summer.

She gives him a concert, right there and then. It's just for him,
because Conor loves music. And musicians do, too.

Carrie's feelings, when she hears about Conor's day, are different. She's cross. *It's not fair.* She sometimes thinks Conor gets too much attention as it is—never mind people doing him favors by introducing him to famous singers. *Not that I wanted to meet Carly Simon anyway…because I'm going to be a writer when I grow up, not a DJ. People don't say, "Oh Carrie, you love words. Here's a famous writer for you to meet."* Carrie decides to spend a lot of time in her room working on the story which will one day make her famous. *Then Conor will get tired of everyone paying attention to me*, she thinks.

Conor wishes Carrie wouldn't be mad. Then he thinks he'll be mad at her for being mad at him. Joan thinks she may get mad at both of them before too long. But she has plans everyone will like: an invitation to a friend's pool.

Yes! Carrie and Conor are in agreement on this idea.

As soon as they get there, as soon as it's polite—one, two, three, everyone jumps into the water. Carrie dives again and again. She's good at it, and she loves it. Brenna sits on the steps counting her toes, getting them wet one at a time. Conor floats and swims with his dad, his mom, his no-longer-cross big sister. There is nowhere, not even in the ocean, where Conor feels so free—*Who cares about muscles?*—as in a pool. Oceans can, and have, knocked him over. But with a little help from a friend, pool water floats him, holds him.

Just as Carrie likes to fly off the diving board, Conor likes to have breath-holding contests. Carrie can't always beat Conor in a breath-holding contest. Conor likes to imagine himself sitting in his chair on the podium someday, waiting to receive his Olympic medal for breath-holding.

Conor spends almost all day in the water. Joan makes him take a break when he starts to shrivel like a raisin. But if someone is willing to go with him, Conor Healy heads right back in again. Lying on the mat in the water, Conor wonders why there aren't any pool songs as great as the beach songs he loves.

Then, as Carrie tries to knock him off, he realizes that today he doesn't much care. More important to make goofy faces than worry. More important to beat Carrie one last time than think about ladies and their ice cream money. More important to try to fit all three kids on one mat than remember Mrs. Nasty Despicable. Tom and Joan try to keep everyone from tipping over.

"Which don't come easy," Tom says.

"Which is a good song," Conor says.

"What a surprise!" Carries says, as she falls off and under, as laughter breaks out, and who cares who was mad at whom?

Like a favorite song, vacation seems as if it's over almost before it's begun. Time on the island is winding down. It's time for fitting in last things. Conor and Carrie want a picnic dinner, so the family heads to Menemsha for a take-out meal at the edge of the water, near boats and beach, with enough time left over for a perfect sunset—a finale.

After worrying about what to have and then ordering the usual, the Healys find the right spot. Conor switches to the blue chair, sitting

down close to the ground with everyone. He doesn't mind that the gulls are providing the evening's music. He joins in trading stories of the summer, who dunked whom, who fell off, and whether Tom has gotten any better at steering the boat.

Carrie tells Conor she hears the Beatles are having a reunion to sing just for him. "Tell them I'm too busy," he says.

Brenna tells everyone to look at a seagull who has just one leg. "Give him a dollar," says Conor.

Having waited till it's almost too late, the Healys race down the dock to see the sunset. Conor thinks he's going off the end of the dock for sure. The light around them turns golden. People, even Brenna, stand quietly as the sun once more slips away. Conor watches with his family, thinking—like the words of a song—*this is where I want to be*. He makes a mental list of songs he would play if someone wanted to dedicate a song to a sunset.

Then Conor Healy turns to his family with an important,

end-of-vacation announce-
ment. "We need ice
cream," he cries, "and I've
got some money for it!"

They all agree. It's the
perfect ending for a
Vineyard day—and a
Vineyard vacation.